TECH TO PROTECT

HIGH-TECH DEFENSE SCIENCE

JAMES BOW

www.crabtreebooks.com

Author: James Bow

Editors: Sarah Eason, John Andrews, and Petrice Custance

Proofreader and indexer: Wendy Scavuzzo

Editorial director: Kathy Middleton

Design: Paul Myerscough, Paul Oakley, and Jane McKenna

Cover design: Paul Myerscough

Photo research: Rachel Blount

Production coordinator and Prepress technician: Margaret Amy Salter

Print coordinator: Margaret Amy Salter

Consultant: David Hawksett

Produced for Crabtree Publishing Company by Calcium Creative.

Photo Credits:

t=Top, tr=Top Right, tl=Top Left, tc=Top Center, b=Bottom, br=Bottom Right, bc=Bottom Center, r=Right, cr=Center Right

BAE Systems: 3, 8; DVIDS: U.S. Air Force photo by Airman 1st Class Donald Hudson 22br, U.S. Air Force photo by Senior Airman Miles Wilson 5t, U.S. Dept. of Defense 20–21, U.S. Marine Corps photo by Sgt. Jessica Quezada 9, Cpl. Garrett White 18b; Lockheed Martin: 23; Shutterstock: 24Novembers 16–17, Kletr 28tc, NEstudio 6–7, Olemac 28br; Wikimedia Commons: 14, Air Force Research Laboratory Directed Energy Directorate Public Affairs Photo released by the U.S. Air Force 24–25, AlexanderAlUS 20b, Boston Dynamics 27, Colin 18–19, DARPA 26, 29b, Didier Descouens 28tl, Divemasterking2000 28bc, Tech. Sgt. Matt Hecht 22cr, Brian A. Jaques 13, Steve Jurvetson 24b, Charles Levy 29t, Francesco Mondada and Michael Bonani 12, National Library NZ 28tr, Noblemouse 27br, Roens 16b, United States Air Force 4–5, U.S. Air Force photo by Paul Ridgeway 1, 15t, U.S. Army 15b, U.S. Navy photo courtesy of General Dynamics Bath Iron Works 10–11, Vvzvlad 6r.

Cover: Wikimedia Commons: DARPA

Library and Archives Canada Cataloguing in Publication

Bow, James, 1972-, author
        Tech to protect / James Bow.

(Techno planet)
Includes index.
Issued in print and electronic formats.
ISBN 978-0-7787-3606-6 (hardcover).--
ISBN 978-0-7787-3620-2 (softcover).--
ISBN 978-1-4271-1994-0 (HTML)

     1. Military weapons--Technological innovations--Juvenile literature.
2. Military supplies--Technological innovations--Juvenile literature.
3. Defense industries--Technological innovations--Juvenile literature.
I. Title.

UF520.B69 2017   j623.4   C2017-903605-X
                                       C2017-903606-8

Library of Congress Cataloging-in-Publication Data

CIP available at the Library of Congress

Crabtree Publishing Company
www.crabtreebooks.com   1-800-387-7650

Printed in Canada/092017/PB20170719

Copyright © **2018 CRABTREE PUBLISHING COMPANY.** All rights reserved. No part of this publication may be reproduced, stored in a retrieval system or be transmitted in any form or by any means, electronic, mechanical, photocopying, recording, or otherwise, without the prior written permission of Crabtree Publishing Company. In Canada: We acknowledge the financial support of the Government of Canada through the Canada Book Fund for our publishing activities.

Published in Canada
Crabtree Publishing
616 Welland Ave.
St. Catharines, Ontario
L2M 5V6

Published in the United States
Crabtree Publishing
PMB 59051
350 Fifth Avenue, 59th Floor
New York, New York 10118

Published in the United Kingdom
Crabtree Publishing
Maritime House
Basin Road North, Hove
BN41 1WR

Published in Australia
Crabtree Publishing
3 Charles Street
Coburg North
VIC, 3058

CONTENTS

Making It Safe	4
Smart Weapons	6
Bigger, Faster, Higher	8
Stealth and Safety	10
Robot Defense	12
Remote Control Defense	14
Someone Is Watching Me	16
Watching the Internet	18
Personal Defense Tech	20
Making Humans Superhuman	22
Changing Defense	24
Future Fantastic	26
Tech Timeline	28
Glossary	30
Learning More	31
Index and About the Author	32

MAKING IT SAFE

On a monitor, a police officer watches a suspicious package lying in the middle of the floor. Someone has called in a threat. The building has been evacuated. People have been warned to stay away by loudspeakers, and also by text messages on their phones. Everyone is safe, but now police must deal with what might be a bomb.

Fortunately, the police officer is not risking her life. She is in another building. Using a remote control, she guides a bomb disposal robot toward the suspicious package.

TECH—FOR BETTER OR WORSE?

Technology makes people's lives easier. Cars and planes make us move faster. Computers and the Internet make us more knowledgeable. Special cameras allow us to see things our eyes cannot. New materials make possible things we could only imagine before. By experimenting, we look for ways to make our tools easier to use and more powerful. As technology changes, so do we. We start to do things differently.

Some of the most important tools we have are the things we use to defend ourselves. New technology can help armies fight wars and police stop criminals. Not all progress is good, however. Weapons are designed to kill. The smarter these weapons become, the more people they are able to kill, sometimes by mistake. Advances in police technology raise questions about our **privacy**. Cameras can look everywhere and see everything. Some people may say that if we have nothing to hide, we have nothing to fear. However, technologies can wind up in the wrong hands and be misused.

SEEING THE ADVANTAGES

Technologies have helped our armies and police forces save lives. New technologies allow officers to stop suspects without killing them. They can help emergency services and governments deal with the aftereffects of war by making bombs safe and the land free of chemicals that could destroy crops. They can use satellites and computer surveillance to watch suspects to prevent crimes from happening before the police get involved.

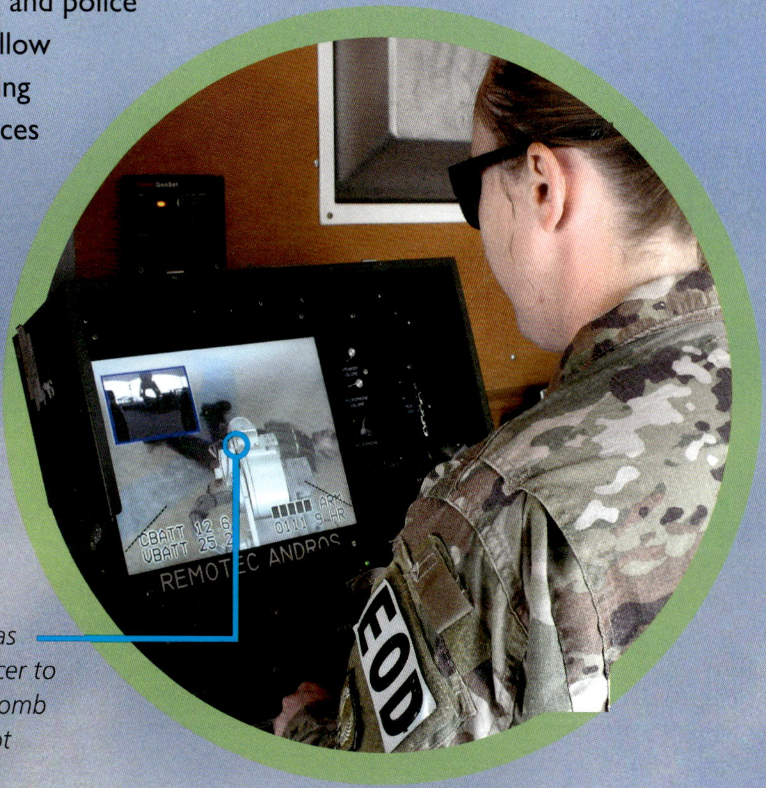

Video cameras allow an officer to see what a bomb disposal robot is seeing.

A F-16 Falcon flies in a military exercise. New technology is tested in drills and simulations that are close to real life.

SMART WEAPONS

Humans have always made and relied on weapons. Today, new technologies are being used to create extremely advanced weapons. These weapons are capable of causing much destruction, but new technology is also helping humans develop ways to limit that destruction.

SMART RIFLES AND BULLETS

Bombs leave a wide destructive path, but **sniper** bullets are more precise. **Lasers** and high-zoom cameras help snipers see and hit targets from far away. British sniper Corporal Craig Harrison holds the record for the longest shot, hitting a target in Afghanistan from 8,120 feet (2,475 m) away. The bullet traveled at 2,093 miles per hour (3,368 kph).

Snipers can hide, but they must see their target to fire their rifle. When they do this, they are placing themselves in danger. One answer is the CornerShot rifle, which bends so it can shoot around corners. It was developed by an ex-officer from the Israeli army. Cameras ensure the soldiers shoot accurately, while staying safely behind a wall.

Even more effective is a bullet that aims itself, like a guided missile. In 2015, the Defense Advanced Research Projects Agency (DARPA) in the United States put this technology in a bullet, allowing it to stay on target even in high winds. Other technology makes sure weapons can fire without jamming. It used to be important to keep your gunpowder dry, but today armies can even fire some rifles underwater.

Although scopes help snipers see their target, they must adjust for wind and gravity. New guided bullets can help.

Soldiers are now able to use apps and computer programs to assist them in the field.

IN THE RIGHT HANDS

One problem with weapons is they can be used against anyone. **Microstamping** technology stamps the identification of a gun onto a bullet. This helps police trace bullets back to a criminal's gun. Better yet, some smart guns can read the DNA of the person using it. If the wrong person's finger is on the trigger, the weapon is turned off.

TECHNO PLANET

Soldiers are able to use apps and computer technology to help them on the battlefield. Nett Warrior is a technology that uses a cell-phone-like device to provide soldiers with up-to-the-minute, accurate battlefield information. On the screen, soldiers can see the location of their fellow soldiers, the location of enemy targets, and whether an area has been cleared as safe. Soldiers can then make quick decisions with less risk of deadly mistakes.

BIGGER, FASTER, HIGHER

People are always looking to make technology faster and more effective. Armed forces do this, too. It often leads to an **arms race**. Many countries rely on the very latest technologies to try to keep their forces stocked with the most advanced planes, ships, and missiles in the world.

HITTING THE RIGHT SPEED

On October 14, 1947, U.S. Air Force pilot Chuck Yeager flew a Bell X-1 rocket plane to 805.6 miles per hour (1,296.5 kph). This was the first time anyone had broken the **sound barrier**. The fastest plane ever was the North American X-15, which reached 4,520 miles per hour (7,274 kph), or 6.7 times the speed of sound. Missiles travel even faster. The Sprint anti-ballistic missile can reach 10 times the speed of sound.

However, fast does not always win wars. BAE Systems, a company in the United Kingdom, is working on a plane called the Transformer. While not super-fast, it is three planes in one. Two planes can detach from the wings to carry out separate missions. They can then return and reattach to the main plane in flight. Joined together, these planes save fuel and travel farther by reducing **drag**.

Armies need to move quickly and easily. The Landing Craft Air Cushion helps them with that. It is a **hovercraft** that can speed across the water on a cushion of air. It also runs onto the land, allowing soldiers to invade a country by sea without being slowed down by the water.

The BAE Systems Transformer would be able to use weapons, drop supplies, and go on spying missions.

SPACE RACE

Armies that hold the high ground have an advantage, and there is nothing higher than space. In the 1950s and 1960s, there was a race between the United States and the **Soviet Union** to be the first into space. Today, satellites in space help planes and other military vehicles find their way. Satellites take pictures and send data that can warn countries of enemy troop movements or attacks. This has led countries to consider using weapons to attack these satellites.

However, countries such as the United States and Russia have agreed not to fire on satellites. So far, weapons have been kept out of space.

Hovercraft can carry more troops and equipment than old landing craft. They can carry soldiers farther onto shore to safe areas away from enemy fire.

STEALTH AND SAFETY

Sometimes the best defense is not to be seen. Armies use **camouflage**, such as special paints or nets, to blend soldiers and vehicles into the background. The Canadian Armed Forces use computer software to create digital camouflage patterns called **CADPAT** (Canadian Disruptive Pattern) that are harder to see, even with night-vision devices.

NOW YOU SEE IT, NOW YOU DON'T

BAE Systems has created a camouflage technology called ADAPTIV. This is a series of hand-sized tiles that cover military vehicles. The tiles are reflective and each one can be heated or cooled. ADAPTIV tricks **infrared** cameras into mistaking tanks for non-military vehicles, such as a car. Some people believe this breaks the rules of war. Making a tank look like a car could make enemy soldiers shoot at anything in case it is a military vehicle in disguise, which could cause harm to many innocent people.

TECHNO PLANET

Police have stealth vehicles, for undercover missions and for catching speeding drivers. These used to be cars with no police markings. This sometimes led to confusion when officers identified themselves. New stealth vehicles have hidden LED lights. These light up to tell you that an officer is pulling you over.

ALMOST INVISIBLE

A technology called **radar** played a big part in World War II. It used radio waves to detect incoming planes. Ever since, people have designed **stealth** planes to try to absorb or **deflect** these waves and fly undetected. The United States Air Force B-21 bomber is the latest stealth plane. Its makers say it can get around the best air defenses. However, Russia claims that its new S-500 air-defense system can destroy stealthy targets up to 125 miles (200 km) away.

PEACEFUL POLICING

Police officers need to be seen by the communities they serve. The lights and sirens on their cars tell drivers to get out of the way while they race to emergencies. New technology is changing these vehicles, too. The sound of a siren can now be aimed in the direction of people who need to hear it. This does not disturb people nearby who might be sleeping.

Military technology has found its way into some police vehicles, including armor and more powerful weapons. This has some people worried. They feel military technology belongs on the battlefield, not in their communities.

The profile of the 600-foot (183-m) long USS Zumwalt destroyer makes it look like a small fishing boat on radar screens.

ROBOT DEFENSE

Sending a robot to do the work of a soldier or a police officer means one less person is put at risk. Britain's Royal Army Ordnance Corps built the first bomb disposal robot in 1972. Bomb disposal robots have video cameras that let officers examine the bomb in safety. Some robots soak bombs with water or carry them somewhere safe to blow them up. **X-ray** scanners can look inside devices without opening them. This allows bomb technicians to see what they are dealing with.

ROBOTS ON THE MARCH

Smarter technology means smarter robots. Some robots are now small enough to go into places that humans cannot. They carry special cameras to detect body heat. They have sensitive microphones that can hear muffled voices and even heartbeats. Robots are also being made to act more like people. Atlas is a robot developed by Boston Dynamics. It walks upright on two legs. It handles uneven **terrain** better than a tank or an armored vehicle. Atlas could soon be walking over rubble, carrying equipment, and keeping up with human soldiers.

Armies and police forces are not limited to single robots. Swarm bots are small robots that communicate with each other and fly in formation. They work together to go into small places. They can help police officers look for suspects who are hiding, or find survivors after an accident.

No single swarm bot is in charge. Each one can finish the job, even if one bot is lost.

12

TECHNO PLANET

Sending a robot into a building when a crime is taking place is less risky than sending in a human. However, until recently, robots have been too large and slow to help police tackle criminals. The Throwbot XT is a small, wheeled robot that can be thrown through the window of a building. It can then move around inside. A video camera and a microphone allow the police to see and hear armed suspects and any innocent civilians. The tiny robot lets the police know exactly what they will find when they enter the building.

Bomb disposal robots have tank treads to move over difficult terrain. Some can even climb stairs.

REMOTE CONTROL DEFENSE

As robotic technology improves, robots will be used more often in place of soldiers and police officers. Drones are special types of robots that fly like a helicopter or a plane. They can be remotely controlled by a human. They can also follow instructions on their own. Drones carry **sensors** and cameras to look around in areas where it may not be safe for people to be. They can even carry missiles and bombs.

DRONES TO THE RESCUE

The military already uses flying drones to take aerial photographs of enemy terrain or to deliver supplies. Urban Aeronautics, a company in Israel, has created the Cormorant. It is a driverless flying car that can slip through narrow streets and hover close to buildings. It can rescue soldiers, police officers, or civilians from the tops of burning buildings.

Drone tanks, such as the U.S. Army vehicle known as Ripsaw, can advance on and fire at enemy soldiers or tanks. They are remote controlled. The people operating the drone tank are not at risk. This also makes it safer for the soldiers who follow up the attack. Drones are **expendable**. This means that they can be shot down without risking the lives of soldiers. However, drones are very expensive, so the military gets upset if one of them is shot down!

Unlike a helicopter, the Cormorant can hover without long blades, making it perfect for getting near buildings.

14

OUT OF CONTROL

Drones are already being used as robot bombs. This makes people very concerned about drones. People argue that killing by remote control makes armies forget or ignore the human cost of war. Drones have accidentally killed dozens of civilians living in or near war zones. Technology has advanced to the point where drones could become **autonomous**. The idea of a robot having the ability to shoot to kill without being controlled by a human has raised many concerns. What if something went wrong and the robot could not be stopped?

There are also worries over the misuse of drones by criminals or terrorists. However, there is already drone technology than can tackle rogue drones. In the Netherlands, police have used some old technology in a new way. They have trained eagles to take down drones. The eagles are fast and know how to catch prey in midair.

The MQ-9 Reaper is an attack drone that can carry four missiles and is operated from the ground.

The Ripsaw drone tank can plant mines, tow vehicles, and carry 5,000 pounds (2,270 kg).

SOMEONE IS WATCHING ME

Soldiers and police do a lot of guard duty. However, people cannot stand on guard all the time. For more than 100 years, cameras have been used to watch places when people could not. Today, many city centers have cameras on every block, and surveillance footage is analyzed using advanced computer technology and satellite systems. Someone is always watching—but should they be?

READING FACES

Today, video cameras are in office buildings, malls, and even on public streets. So much is filmed, but humans cannot possibly watch it all. In the 1960s, computer scientists programmed a computer to identify human faces out of a selection of pictures. As the technology advanced, computers recognized faces faster. Now, computers can recognize individual faces in crowds and track individuals through multiple camera feeds. Police have been able to find many people and solve many cases using this technology.

However, because cameras see everything, people are worried about their privacy. Police can make mistakes and accuse the wrong people, even with camera evidence. **Hackers** might steal the images and use them for **identity theft**. A government might spy on people who are worried about how that government is operating.

Surveillance cameras can be hacked. This fiber-optic splitter can tap into a camera feed and steal images.

EVERY ANGLE COVERED

To deal with attacks against U.S. soldiers in Iraq, BAE Systems invented the Autonomous Real-Time Ground Ubiquitous Surveillance Imaging System (ARGUS-IS). Drones took aerial photographs every second, logging up to 24 hours of images. When a bomb went off, officials looked back through the images to see when the bomb was planted, what vehicle was used to plant the bomb, and where the bomb came from. However, plans to introduce the system in Dayton, Ohio, to help police were stopped when residents objected. Do the police have the right to look down at your back yard, regardless of whether you are doing anything wrong?

There are more than 350 million surveillance cameras installed around the world. New York City's Domain Awareness System uses 6,000 cameras.

TECHNO PLANET

Thanks to satellite technology, police can now track vehicles they cannot even see. The StarChase system allows police cars to catch vehicles more safely. A police car uses a laser to attach a **Global Positioning System (GPS)** tag on an escaping vehicle. The police then track the vehicle on a computer and intercept it wherever it stops. It means the police can stop the vehicle without a high-speed chase that could endanger the driver and innocent bystanders.

WATCHING THE INTERNET

The Internet is an important tool. Like all tools, it can be used in good and bad ways. The way we can be **anonymous** on the Internet can be used for good, such as when people can work together for human rights against harsh governments. However, being anonymous can also allow criminals and terrorists to plan dangerous things out of sight of authorities.

SPREADING VIRUSES

The Internet is a tempting target for terrorists and criminals. Computer viruses can spread through e-mails or websites. They steal or erase people's files. Trojan horses are **malicious** computer programs. They use virus e-mails or fake websites to trick users into handing over passwords. Malicious hackers can hijack computers and use Trojan horses to overwhelm websites with fake traffic, shutting down business or government websites.

In 2000, the ILOVEYOU computer virus spread to more than 50 million computers in 10 days. It caused more than $20 billion in damage. In 2016, the Tiny Banker Trojan horse infected banking websites to grab customer passwords. Security experts worry that viruses are already being written to target a country's **infrastructure**, such as computers in power plants and water treatment plants. Losing access to power and clean water could be disastrous for a community.

*Around the world, police and security forces employ more than a million people to fight **cybercrime**.*

FIGHTING BACK

Police departments have formed cybercrime units to try to stop people from using the Internet to commit crimes. The technology company IBM has built a facility called the X-Force Command. This acts like large government or corporate computer systems, so that friendly, or "white hat," hackers can test cyber security by trying to hack in. Security forces use programs that monitor e-mails as they pass through the Internet. They search for keywords and patterns that suggest a threat. These forces use their own viruses and Trojan horses to **infiltrate** terrorist websites.

However, people worry about how much the police and armed forces can and should do. New technology can fall into the wrong hands. Data can be released accidentally. Think of all the e-mails you have sent and all the sites you have visited online. Not all e-mails and social media posts should be shared. Sometimes they can be embarrassing, and some have even gotten people fired from jobs.

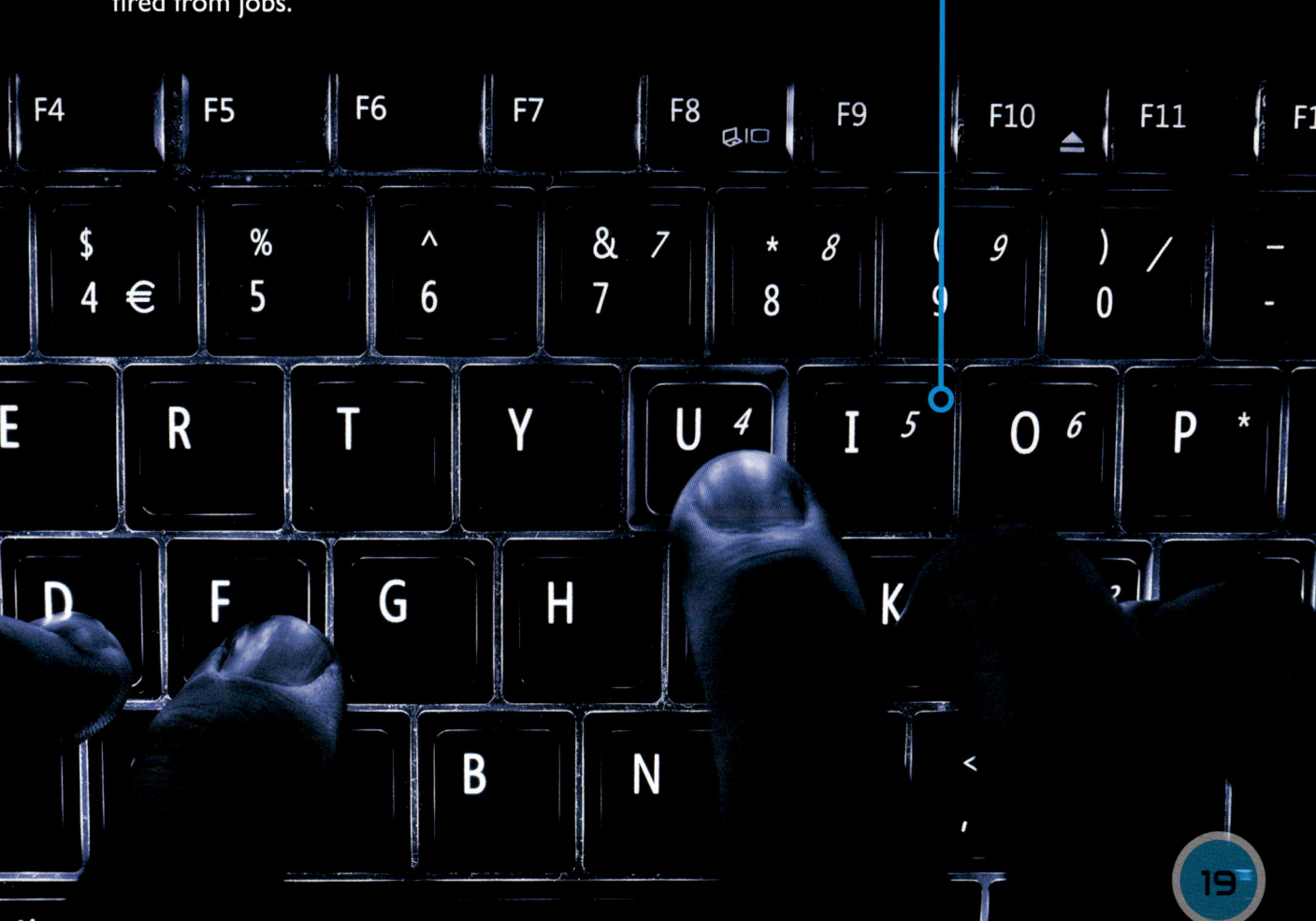

A virus downloaded on a victim's computer can lock the keyboard, and hackers then demand money to unlock it.

PERSONAL DEFENSE TECH

Suits of armor became useless once guns came along. Then, in 1964, a chemist created Kevlar—a strong plastic thread that can be woven into a fabric that stops bullets. Today, scientists are working on even stronger materials. Graphene, made out of carbon **atoms**, is extremely light yet 200 times stronger than steel. Liquid body armor uses Kevlar that is soaked in a chemical fluid. The Kevlar fibers hold this fluid, and when struck by a bullet, the fluid hardens into a solid in milliseconds. You need 20 to 40 layers of Kevlar to stop a bullet, which makes Kevlar armor stiff and heavy. Liquid body armor is much lighter and more flexible.

HEALING ARMOR

Armor is not just about stopping bullets. During the American occupation of Iraq, United States Marines coated their gas tanks with a new "self-healing" plastic. This plastic contained pockets of liquid that turned solid when exposed to air. Before, bullets shot through metal gas tanks left holes that leaked gasoline. With this smart armor, bullets still passed through the fuel tanks, but the plastic sealed up behind them, leaving no leaks. This saved lives.

INVISIBLE ARMOR

The best armor might be to not be seen at all. Planes and other military or police equipment may one day no longer need camouflage. Scientists are working on ways to bend light around objects, so that sensors see what is behind an object rather than the object itself. Devices already exist that can bend **microwaves** around objects. Once scientists achieve this with visible light, an incoming plane would be undetectable by sensors.

This honeycomb of carbon atoms provides great strength in a tiny space and is incredibly light.

Most U.S. soldiers carry at least 60 pounds (27 kg) of gear. All armies are interested in technologies that lighten this load.

TECHNO PLANET

New technologies help keep soldiers more comfortable in the field. By adding magnetic particles to the fluid in **shock absorbers**, and using computer-controlled magnets, armies can adjust how military vehicles react to different terrain. This means they can smooth out the ride. The U.S. Army has also created a battery-powered personal heater and air conditioner, called the Light-Weight Environmental Control System. Soldiers wear it under body armor to keep cool in deserts and warm in cold places. Making soldiers comfortable helps them stay alert, and better able to spot enemies and dangerous situations.

MAKING HUMANS SUPERHUMAN

Robots can be stronger and faster than humans. They can see what humans cannot. However, robots are still a long way from replacing soldiers or police officers. Instead, wearable technologies can give our soldiers and police officers robot-like powers.

SEEING MORE CLEARLY

Night-vision goggles help soldiers and police officers see dark areas as though they were in daylight. These goggles have sensors that take in all the light we can see. They also take in infrared light, which we cannot see. A computer reads this data and shows it on the inside of the goggles. Some devices shoot out infrared beams to add to the brightness.

There are also sensors that can pick up even more light that we cannot see, including **ultraviolet** light and X-rays. Computers take this data and change it into colors that humans can see and understand. Infrared sensors on satellites help map terrain and soil conditions faster than human mapmakers. The sensors can help soldiers find enemy camps in the jungle, or help police find criminal hideouts.

Just as radios keep soldiers and police officers in touch with their command centers, wearable computers allow for silent communication. Special goggles can display messages right in front of a soldier's eyes. Companies such as Google are also working on software that can translate foreign language signs. The translation would display on a screen in the viewer's own language, which would be great for soldiers in a foreign country. It would also be great for tourists!

High-tech night-vision goggles can deal with sudden flashes of light so they do not blind the soldier on patrol.

GETTING STRONGER

As well as super vision, new technology will give soldiers super strength. **Exoskeletons** help people with disabilities move again. They can also help and protect soldiers. Lockheed Martin has developed the Human Universal Load Carrier (HULC) exoskeleton for the U.S. Army. Soldiers can wear the exoskeleton to help them carry heavy objects over long distances—without breaking a sweat. Combine this with lightweight materials such as graphene or spider silk, and you have the makings of a suit of armor that stops bullets and gives the wearer incredible strength. It may even let them fly. The company JetPack International has successfully tested jet packs that can fly as high as 10,000 feet (3,048 m).

Exoskeletons can also be used by firefighters and police forces.

CHANGING DEFENSE

Technology exists that can stop attackers without killing them. Tasers shoot a pair of metal darts that stick to the skin and deliver an electric shock, causing targets to lose control of their muscles. Tactical pens are made from ultra-tough metal. They work as a pen, but they have strong enough tips to break glass and cause enough injury to stop an attacker. The United States Marine Corps has tested guns that shoot out streams of sticky foam to stop people in their tracks.

CROWD CONTROL

Other non-lethal weapons have been developed to deal with large, angry crowds. The PHASR zaps laser lights at targets, temporarily blinding them. The Thunder Generator produces shockwaves of sound and pressure. This can knock people off their feet up to 300 feet (90 m) away. The U.S. military has designed an Active Denial System. This is a microwave ray that creates a burning sensation on the skin. However, non-lethal weapons are not perfect. They can harm and be misused. There are worries about these technologies being used against innocent people participating in peaceful **protests**.

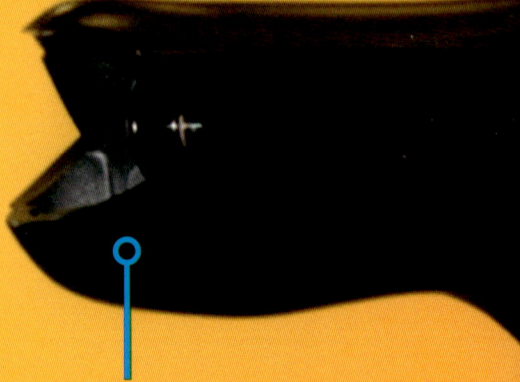

The PHASR laser weapon disables rather than kills an enemy by causing only temporary blindness.

These leaves turn red when they detect nitrogen dioxide, something that is common in explosives.

NATURAL DEFENSE

Scientists are now experimenting with plant technology as a form of defense. In 2004, Danish company Aresa Biodetection created a new kind of plant. Its leaves changed color when its roots detected explosive materials. This plant saved lives by showing people where mines were in a battlefield long after the soldiers had left. In 2016, engineers from the Massachusetts Institute of Technology (MIT) planted tiny tubes of carbon, called nanotubes, in the leaves of spinach plants. The leaves change color as soon as they sniff nearby explosives. This plant technology could be used around airports or government offices to stop terrorists.

*When wars stop, ammunition is left behind. It poisons plants and animals for years afterward. The U.S. Army is looking at making its munitions out of **biodegradable** plastic. This would make bullets less toxic, or poisonous. The bullets might also contain seeds. These could grow into plants that would clean up the soil. Biodegradable ammunition can help people rebuild more easily once peace comes.*

TECHNO PLANET

25

FUTURE FANTASTIC

Technology is neither good nor evil. It depends on how we use it. Weapons are designed to harm and kill. They can do terrible damage in the wrong hands. However, much of the technology we depend on now was first created for military use. GPS satellite technology helped soldiers in the field to locate where they were. Today, GPS helps us get to where we are going. Radar was invented to detect enemy planes. Now, radar detects thunderstorms and tornadoes. The Internet was first designed as a way for the U.S. military to keep communicating after a nuclear attack. Today, the Internet is an important tool that connects people around the world.

CHANGING THE RULES

Every year, technology pushes the boundaries of what is possible. The United States Department of Defense is already working on a self-steering bullet, called EXACTO, which can change direction. Plane makers Boeing and Northrop Grumman are developing fighter jets that will fly with no pilots. People will operate tanks far from the battlefield on a computer—almost like a video game. Soldiers will wear **augmented reality** headsets that allow them to see much more than the naked eye can see.

Computers and robots will have a bigger role in our military and police forces. Artificial intelligences will spot things on cameras and in online activity that most humans would miss. We will invent ever stronger and lighter materials. We will continue to build technologies that help humans do superhuman things.

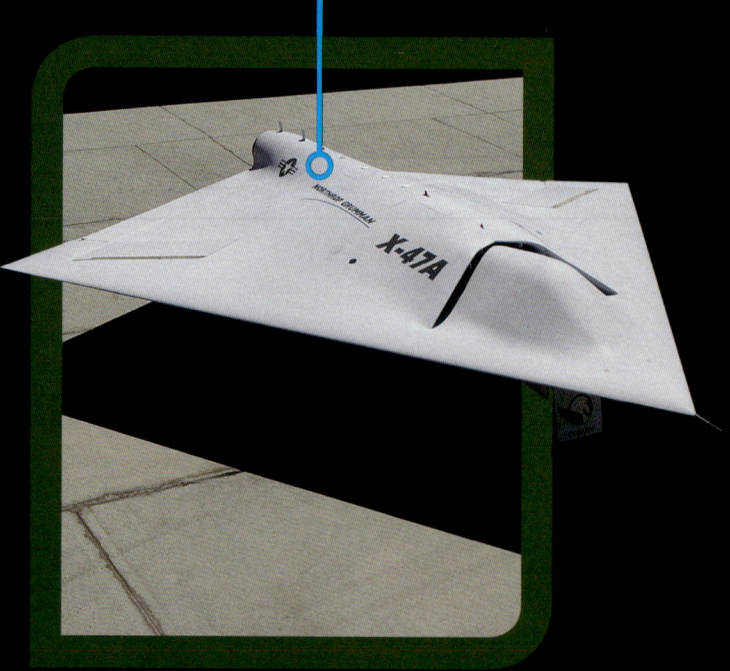

In the future, unmanned planes will be more than drones. They will be able to do the work of fighter jets.

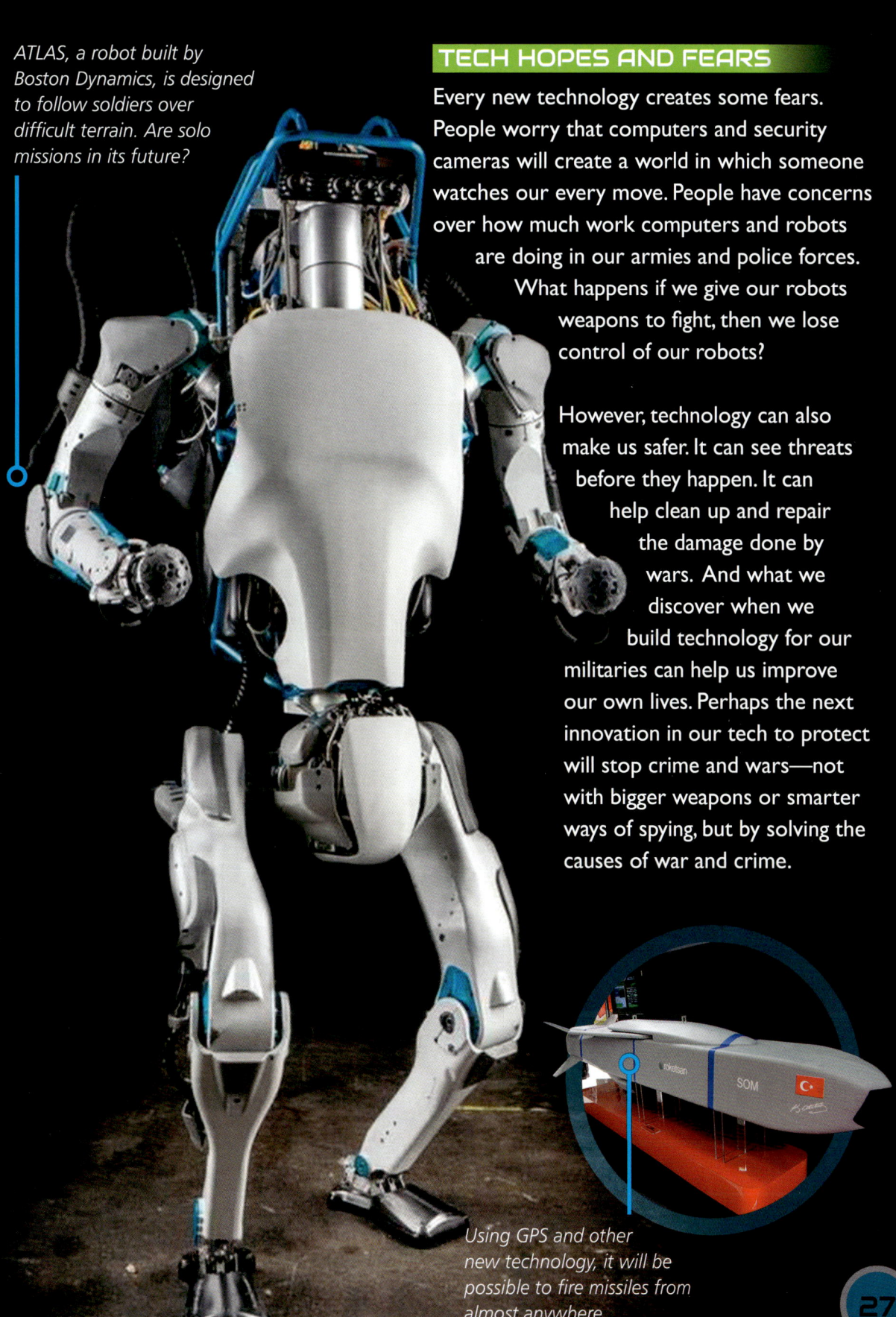

ATLAS, a robot built by Boston Dynamics, is designed to follow soldiers over difficult terrain. Are solo missions in its future?

TECH HOPES AND FEARS

Every new technology creates some fears. People worry that computers and security cameras will create a world in which someone watches our every move. People have concerns over how much work computers and robots are doing in our armies and police forces. What happens if we give our robots weapons to fight, then we lose control of our robots?

However, technology can also make us safer. It can see threats before they happen. It can help clean up and repair the damage done by wars. And what we discover when we build technology for our militaries can help us improve our own lives. Perhaps the next innovation in our tech to protect will stop crime and wars—not with bigger weapons or smarter ways of spying, but by solving the causes of war and crime.

Using GPS and other new technology, it will be possible to fire missiles from almost anywhere.

27

TECH TIMELINE

20,000 B.C.E. Earliest evidence of arrowheads

500 B.C.E. China develops the trebuchet—a catapult that can hurl a rock 410 feet (125 m)

1132 China develops the first cannon

1836 American Samuel Colt invents a "revolving gun," later named the revolver, which could reload much faster than a musket

1916 The first tank goes into battle, in World War I

400,000 B.C.E. Earliest evidence of spears

5,000 B.C.E. The first metal daggers and swords, made from bronze

800 China develops gunpowder, leading to the earliest gun and the first rockets

1775 The first submarine, called the Turtle, is invented by American David Bushnell

1851 The first machine gun is invented

28

1945
The first atomic bomb is dropped on Hiroshima, Japan

1974
The Taser is invented

1997
The United States tests an anti-satellite laser

2002
The United States Central Intelligence Agency (CIA) uses the unmanned Predator drone for the first time, striking a target in Afghanistan

2016
The company Nett Warrior develops a military cell phone app to allow American soldiers to call in air strikes

1941
The G-suit, designed to help pilots handle forces from rapid acceleration, is invented by Canadian Wilbur Franks

1968
The city of Olean, New York, installs the first security cameras on its main street to fight crime

1986
The first unauthorized computer virus is created, infecting IBM computers

2002
The CADPAT, a digital camouflage system, is invented by the Canadian Forces

2013
Boston Dynamics delivers the Atlas robot to the United States Defense Advanced Research Projects Agency (DARPA)

29

GLOSSARY

Please note: Some **bold-faced** words are defined where they appear in the book.

anonymous Doing something without telling anybody your name

arms race When two or more militaries race to produce the biggest or most powerful armed forces

atoms The smallest parts of a substance

augmented reality A digitally enhanced version of reality

autonomous Able to assess its surroundings and make its own decisions

biodegradable Able to be broken down into small parts by natural actions

camouflage Colors and shapes used to blend something in with its background

cybercrime Electronic crime

deflect Cause to change direction

drag The force of the air a plane pushes against when flying

exoskeletons Hard external coverings for the body

expendable Meant to be used up

Global Positioning System (GPS) A way of navigating using satellite signals

hackers People who illegally interfere with information on a computer system

hovercraft A vehicle that moves just above the surface of land or water on a cushion of air

identity theft Using a person's name, address, and other personal details to steal money or goods

infiltrate Sneak into something unnoticed

infrared Invisible light beyond the red end of the color spectrum

infrastructure The systems, such as power, that make things work in a city or country

lasers Devices that produce a narrow and powerful beam of light

malicious Wanting to harm

microstamping Identifying with a tiny mark

microwaves Short waves of energy beyond infrared that we cannot see

privacy Not being seen by other people

protests Gatherings where people show their disapproval of something

sensors Devices that can be placed in something to send information

shock absorbers Devices that soak up sudden amounts of energy

sniper A soldier trained to shoot at individual targets from a far distance

sound barrier The resistance the air creates when an aircraft nears the speed of sound

Soviet Union A country that existed in eastern Europe and northern Asia until 1991—the biggest part is now Russia

stealth Designed to avoid detection

terrain What the ground around you is like

ultraviolet Invisible light beyond the violet end of the color spectrum

X-ray A powerful invisible ray that is similar to light and can pass through some solids

LEARNING MORE

BOOKS

Forrest, Glen C. *Police Technology: 21st-Century Crime-Fighting Tools* (Law Enforcement and Intelligence Gathering). Britannica Educational in Association with Rosen Educational Services, 2017.

Gray, Judy Silverstein, and Taylor Baldwin Kiland. *Cyber Technology: Using Computers to Fight Terrorism* (Military Engineering in Action). Enslow, 2016.

Greve, Tom. *Police: Protect and Serve* (Emergency Response). Rourke Educational Media, 2014.

Herweck, Diana. *Police Officer* (All in a Day's Work). Teacher Created Materials, 2013.

WEBSITES

http://encyclopedia.kids.net.au/page/mi/Military_technology
Information on all kinds of military technology, from ancient weapons to modern cyber warfare.

www.howstuffworks.com
Discover how stealth bombers, Trojan horses, and other defense and attack technologies work—simply key the name into the search box.

http://kinooze.com/who-are-hackers
Find out more about hackers and computer crime.

www.stem-works.com
Learn about science, technology, engineering, and math through dozens of fun activities, including robotics.

INDEX

Active Denial System 24
ADAPTIV 10
apps and computer technology 6, 7, 29
ARGUS-IS 17
armor, body 20–21, 23
armored vehicles 11, 12
arrowheads 28
Atlas robot 12, 27, 29
atomic bomb 29
autonomous drones 15

B-21 bomber plane 11
BAE Systems 8, 10, 17
Bell X-1 rocket plane 8
bending light 20
biodegradable munitions 25
biodetection 24, 25
body armor 20–21, 23
bomb disposal 4, 5, 12, 13
bullets 6–7, 20, 25, 26

CADPAT 10, 29
camouflage technology 10–11, 20, 29
computer viruses 18–19, 29
Cormorant flying car drone 14
CornerShot rifles 6
crime/criminals 4, 5, 7, 13, 15, 18, 19, 22, 27, 29
cybercrime 18–19

daggers and swords 28
DARPA 6
Domain Awareness System 17
drones 14–15, 17, 26

EXACTO 26
exoskeletons 21

F-16 Falcon planes 5
facial recognition technology 16

G-suit 29
GPS technology 17, 26, 27
graphene 20, 23
gunpowder 28

hackers 16, 18, 19
healing armor 20
hovercraft 8, 9
Human Universal Load Carrier (HULC) 23

IBM X-Force Command 19
infrared technology 10, 22
Internet 18–19, 26
invisible armor 20

jet packs 23

Kevlar 20

Landing Craft Air Cushion 8
lasers 6, 17, 24, 29
Light-Weight Environmental Control System 21
liquid body armor 20

machine guns 28
microstamping bullets 7
microwaves 20, 24
military technology 6–7, 8, 9, 10, 11, 14–15, 20–23, 26, 27, 29
missiles 8, 14, 15, 27
MQ-9 Reaper drone 15

Nett Warrior 7, 29
night-vision goggles 22

PHASRs 24
planes 5, 8, 11, 20, 26
plants that detect explosives 24, 25
police technology 4, 5, 10, 11, 16–17, 19, 22, 23, 26, 27
privacy concerns 4, 16

radar 11, 26
rifles 6
Ripsaw drone tank 15
Russia 9, 11

satellites 5, 9, 22, 26, 29
security cameras 27, 29

sign translation device 22
sirens 11
smart bullets 6, 26
smart guns 7
snipers 6
spider silk 23
StarChase system 17
stealth planes 11
stealth vehicles 10
submarines 28
surveillance 5, 16–17, 27
swarm bots 12

tactical pens 24
tanks 10, 12, 14, 15, 26, 28
tasers 24, 29
terrorists 15, 18, 19, 25
Throwbot XT 13
Thunder Generator 24
tracking vehicles 17
Transformer planes 8
Trojan horses 18

USS *Zumwalt* 10–11

video cameras 5, 13, 16

wars 4, 5, 8, 10, 11, 15, 25, 27
weapons 4, 6–7, 8, 9, 11, 24–25, 26, 27, 28

X-15 planes 8

About the Author

James Bow is a writer of more than 40 books for young readers. Born in Toronto, he attended the University of Waterloo, studying urban and regional planning. He currently lives in the city of Kitchener with his wife Erin, and daughters Vivian and Nora.